The
Borrowed
Puppy

Other titles by Holly Webb

The Borrowed Puppy

Holly Webb

Illustrated by Sophy Williams

LITTLE TIGER

LONDON

For all the amazing dog lovers who borrow dogs
every day

LITTLE TIGER
An imprint of the Little Tiger Press Limited
1 Coda Studios, 189 Munster Road, London SW6 6AW

Imported into the EEA by Penguin Random House Ireland,
Morrison Chambers, 32 Nassau Street, Dublin D02 YH68

www.littletiger.co.uk

A paperback original
First published in Great Britain in 2023

ISBN: 978-1-78895-564-5

The Forest Stewardship Council® (FSC®) is a global, not-for-profit
organization dedicated to the promotion of responsible forest management
worldwide. FSC defines standards based on agreed principles for
responsible forest stewardship that are supported by environmental, social,
and economic stakeholders. To learn more, visit www.fsc.org

Chapter One

"Jade. Jade. I want the dogs."

"I'm doing my homework," Jade pointed out as Toby shoved his book on top of her maths worksheet.

"Pleeeaaaase. Dog book."

Jade sighed. She would actually like a break. "Only once though," she warned her little brother. The dog picture book was Toby's absolute favourite, and he'd beg for it over and over until Jade or Dad agreed to read it to him. "I've got to get this maths done. And it's nearly time for dinner – Dad's cooking pasta."

Toby wriggled into Jade's lap, sighing happily as she opened the book. It had been read so many times that the cover was starting to come away from the pages. Toby had lots of books – most of them passed down from Jade – but none of them had been loved as much as this one.

Jade leaned her chin against Toby's soft hair and started to read. She'd read the story so often she almost knew it off by heart – and so did Toby, even though he was only four.

"Good dog," Toby said blissfully as they reached the last page. "Again!"

"You tell it to yourself," Jade suggested. "I've got to finish my maths before dinner."

"Agaaain!" Toby wailed.

"Hey, Toby…" Dad appeared in the kitchen doorway. "Want to help me set the table? Carry the knives and forks for me?"

Toby nodded. He loved helping. Jade thought it made him feel grown up. He trotted importantly into the kitchen and Dad smiled at Jade.

"Thanks, love. You finish off that homework. Dinner will be ready in five minutes."

Jade plugged her fingers in her ears and tried to concentrate on the numbers on her worksheet, while Dad and Toby laid the other end of the table for dinner. She'd got an answer for the last question by the time Dad put the pasta and tomato sauce on the table – it would have to do, even though she wasn't convinced it added up properly.

Toby kept chattering about dogs all the way through dinner, and he persuaded Dad to read him the dog book again as his bedtime story. After she'd put the plates in the kitchen, Jade settled down on the sofa with a sigh.

It would be so nice to have a real dog instead of just reading about them…

She'd asked Dad if they could have a dog but he'd told her it would be just too difficult. Jade's mum had died not long after Toby was born, so Dad had to look after both of them *and* have a job. Although it was getting a bit easier now that Toby had started nursery, Dad said he didn't have time to take care of anyone else, and he'd shaken his head when Jade promised she'd do everything the dog needed. It wasn't as easy as that, he said.

He'd also pointed out that Toby was a bit too young for them to have a dog in the house. If Toby was messing around and accidentally hurt the dog, it might bite because it was scared.

They couldn't risk that. And dogs were expensive too, with food and vet bills…

Jade sighed again, thinking about it all. She supposed Dad was right, but it didn't seem very fair – she was sure they would be brilliant dog owners. Toby loved dogs just as much as she did. Jade had the TV on when Dad came downstairs, but she was still daydreaming about having a dog of her very own.

Dad sat next to her on the sofa, half watching the TV and half frowning at the laptop he had open on his knee. Jade glanced at what he was doing but it didn't look very exciting. He was on the local swap site, trying to find someone who wanted Toby's old pushchair. He was too tall for it now, and his feet dragged on the floor. Plus, he walked everywhere anyway. Dad was uploading photos of the pushchair. It looked a bit battered, Jade thought.

"What's that?" She leaned over, suddenly interested. There was a photo of a dog on the website, jumbled in among all the toys and wardrobes and children's clothes. "Is somebody trying to swap a dog?"

Dad looked at it too. "Not quite. It's an ad for a website called Love My Pup, it helps dog owners find people who might like to help with their dogs."

"What sort of help?" Jade asked curiously.

"Um… Walking mostly, I think. So if the dog owner has to be out at work all day, they ask if someone would like to walk their dog at lunchtime, perhaps. Or just take them home and spend some time with them. Dogs get lonely by themselves. The people who take them love dogs but maybe can't have a dog of their own, so this means they can have one for a little bit."

"But – but –" Jade was so excited she was gabbling. Her words spilled out on top of each other. "That's like us! It's us, Dad! We can't have a dog because Toby's too little and you're too busy working and looking after us. But maybe we could borrow a dog! Could we? Please?"

Dad blinked. He looked really shocked but Jade didn't understand why. It seemed obvious to her that they were the perfect people to sign up to the Love My Pup website. They always went for long walks at the weekends, either in the woods, or by the sea – they had to stop for snacks a lot, and the walks always had a playground in them somewhere, but Jade didn't think a dog would mind having a rest while Toby went on the swings.

"I don't know if we're the sort of

people they're looking for," Dad said slowly. "I don't think they mean children…"

"But why not?" Jade asked, pleading. "We like walking! We're fun! A dog would love us!"

Dad looked thoughtful. "I suppose maybe a friendly sort of dog. Not nervous. Not too big…"

"Yes!" Jade said eagerly. She could just imagine the dog now, racing ahead of her along the sandy beach, or snuffling eagerly at squirrels in the woods. "Please can we sign up, Dad? Please?"

Dad frowned at the screen for a moment and then he nodded. "All right. But this doesn't mean we're definitely going to be matched with a dog, Jade. It could take a while – and we might never get a dog to walk. It'll depend on there being somebody close by who needs help. Just don't get too excited, all right?"

It was all very well for Dad to tell Jade she shouldn't get too excited. But how could she not? Dad had signed them up to the Love My Pup website, and they might finally be getting a dog – well, almost. It wouldn't be their *own* dog, of course, but they'd still be able to take it for walks and play with it. Jade could *pretend* it was theirs, just for a bit.

She raced out of school every day hoping someone had contacted Dad through the Love My Pup website with a dog for them to look after. But after a whole week of waiting, Jade was starting to lose hope.

"I did say it might take a while," Dad said gently, seeing Jade's face fall when he picked her up on Friday afternoon.

"I know… It's just – it sounded so perfect for us," Jade murmured. "I really want to run along the beach with a dog. Wouldn't that be great?" She sighed, and Dad put his arm round her and gave her a hug.

"It would be brilliant. We just need to be patient, that's all. Are you hungry? What shall we have for a snack when we get home? We could make smoothies? There's some strawberries going a bit squishy in the fridge."

Dad was trying to distract her, Jade could tell. "Maybe," she said, trying not to sound miserable. It wasn't Dad's fault there wasn't a dog nearby needing walks. She smiled at him and listened to Toby telling her all about the dinosaurs and mud he'd played with at nursery that morning.

Back at home, Dad started finding the fruit they needed for the smoothies while Jade went upstairs to change out of her uniform. She was dawdling – it was the weekend, there was no hurry – when Dad yelled from downstairs.

"Hey! Jade! Come down here, quick!"

Jade dragged her sweatshirt over her head and made for the stairs. "Sorry. Was I taking ages? What is it?" she added, seeing the huge grin on Dad's face. "What are you looking like that for?"

"Guess!"

Jade gulped excitedly. "Not … not a dog?" she whispered.

"Yes, a dog!"

"For us?" Jade's voice was squeaky with excitement now.

"A little Golden Retriever puppy called Milo." Dad held out his phone to show her. "Look at him! Isn't he beautiful?"

"Oh, wow…" Jade took the phone, cradling it in both hands. The puppy was gorgeous, and it was a great photo too. She could see the feathery fur around his ears, the bright sparkle in his dark eyes. She almost wanted to stroke Dad's phone. "That's like my dream dog, Dad. Exactly the dog I would have wished for. I can't believe we're really going to meet him!"

Chapter Two

Dad had arranged to visit Caroline, Milo's owner, after school on Monday. Jade was a bit surprised he was taking her and Toby too.

"I wanted her to meet you as well," Dad explained as they walked to Caroline's house. She didn't live far from them, just a couple of roads away. "You and Toby are both going to be spending time with Milo, it's not just me. And it was you who suggested we sign up to Love My Pup!"

"I suppose we do need to get to know Milo," Jade agreed. "I mean – it's him we're going to be walking, not his owner!"

Dad nodded. "Don't worry, though. Caroline's description on the website said he was really friendly and that he likes children. Ah, look, here we are – number thirty-six."

Jade could hear squeaky woofing as they walked up the path to the front door, and her heart jumped inside her chest. She was suddenly very nervous and very excited all at once.

"He sounds happy to meet us," she whispered, looking up anxiously at

Dad. "That's a happy barking, isn't it?"

"Sounds like it to me," Dad said firmly.

Jade noticed that Toby was squashing up against Dad's legs and his eyes had gone all round and worried.

"Remember, Milo's only little. Littler than you," Dad said to Toby. "And he might be a bit bouncy. But just stand still, and make sure you keep Rabbit out of his way, OK? He might think Rabbit is for him."

Toby nodded, hugging his old toy rabbit very tight. Dad had tried to persuade him not to bring it, but Rabbit went everywhere Toby did.

The barking got suddenly louder as the door opened and a wild flurry of wagging tail and damp nose came rushing out – or tried to. Caroline was holding on to Milo's collar and she gently pulled him back.

"Sorry about this! He just loves visitors so much. I'm teaching him not to jump up, but it's going slowly! Milo, sit." She smiled at Jade and Toby. "We have to not make a fuss of him until he sits nicely, you see."

Milo whined, still reaching towards

the exciting visitors, but eventually he sat down. His tail was still swooshing from side to side across the floor. Caroline gave him a treat from her pocket and he gobbled it up eagerly.

"He's so beautiful," Jade told Caroline. She was feeling a bit shy but she had to say it.

"Isn't he?" Caroline nodded. "He's four months old now. A real little treasure. Come on in. I can make some tea or coffee? And I've got juice?"

They settled at the table in Caroline's kitchen, Jade and Toby drinking juice and watching Milo roll around the floor with a rope toy. He seemed to really love it – he kept shaking it and making funny little growling noises.

"He's a lovely colour," Dad said. "A sort of reddish brown. Really unusual."

"Yes, he's a red Golden Retriever," Caroline explained. "I'd been thinking about getting a dog for a while and then a friend's dog was having puppies. I fell in love with Milo when I went to see them."

"Jade and Toby would love to have a dog of their own," Dad said. "But Toby's a bit too young for that. This seems like a great way for them to spend time with a puppy."

"Oh, Dad, look!" Jade whispered. Milo had stopped wrestling with his rope toy, and instead he was standing next to Jade's chair, looking up at her hopefully as though he was trying to give the toy to her.

"He wants you to pull the other end," Caroline said, smiling. "He loves that game."

Jade took hold of the rope toy – it was a bit damp and sticky from Milo chewing on it, but she didn't mind – and pulled. Milo let out a play-growl and tugged back hard – much

harder than Jade had been expecting.
"Oooooh, he nearly pulled me off the
chair!" she said, giggling, and giving the
toy a hard tug back.

Milo wriggled and yapped. He seemed delighted with the game. Caroline looked pleased too.

"I'm so glad you got in touch with me. Milo would play like that all day if he could. I've been working from home but I'm back in the office a couple of days a week now, and I've been worrying about him." Caroline sighed. "He chewed up the end of the sofa last week. And I can see why – he doesn't understand why I'm not there to look after him! He must have been really bored. A walk with you a couple of times a week would be great."

"We'd love that. And Toby and I could pop by and spend some time with him at lunchtime on the days you're at work, if that would help," Dad suggested.

Milo dropped the rope toy and leaned against Jade's legs, panting a bit.

"You've worn him out," Dad said, grinning.

Jade rubbed Milo's feathery ears and smiled as he licked her fingers and then closed his eyes, slumping against her like a saggy teddy bear. She looked round at Dad and Caroline hopefully. "Can we start tomorrow?"

Milo stuck out one paw and dragged his rope toy a bit closer. It was his favourite thing and he liked to know where it was. He didn't think the new people were going to take it but he was being careful, just in case.

He leaned back against the girl's legs, closing his eyes blissfully as she rubbed his ears. That felt so nice. She smelled good too – like outdoors and woods and the beach and walks. Caroline had taken him on a long walk early that morning. He'd raced up and down the beach and found a pile of smelly seaweed and a dead crab, but Caroline hadn't wanted him to eat it. Milo came home and snoozed all morning but he'd been starting to feel like he needed another walk until the girl came to play. He got that skittish feeling, like he needed to run or scratch or dig holes in the carpet by the stairs. But he wasn't supposed to do that…

Milo licked the girl's fingers and heard her giggle.

Then he yawned hugely, showing small white puppy teeth. The girl was scratching under his chin and he leaned his head back, pointing his nose straight up to the ceiling. That was just the right place, the itchy spot, right there. He was so 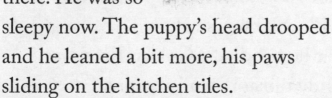 sleepy now. The puppy's head drooped and he leaned a bit more, his paws sliding on the kitchen tiles.

He was asleep.

Chapter Three

The next day at school crept by. Jade
kept stopping to gaze out of the
window and remember all over again
that at the end of the day she, Dad and
Toby would be off to the woods with
Milo. She was so excited.

She doodled a Golden Retriever
on her history worksheet and drew
little paw prints on the back of her

hand when they were supposed to
be listening in literacy. She spent
break and lunchtime telling everyone
about Milo – how sweet and funny
and beautiful he was. By their last
lesson that afternoon she could hardly
concentrate at all – she just kept
staring at the tree in the corner of
the playground and thinking about
how much more fun racing along her
favourite path in the woods was going
to be with a puppy running beside her.

Then her friend Arthur kicked
her under the table and Jade jumped,
remembering where she was. "What
was that for?" she whispered crossly,
rubbing her ankle.

"Miss Carson was watching you!"
Arthur pointed out, jerking his head

towards their teacher. Luckily she'd been distracted by someone else getting stuck on their division problems, but Jade realized Arthur was right. Miss Carson had already told her off about drawing on her hands. She definitely didn't want to get into trouble today – what if Miss Carson had to come out and talk to Dad, and that meant they couldn't take Milo for a walk!

"Thanks," she whispered to Arthur, then she scowled down at her maths book. Only twenty minutes of school left. That was all.

Jade raced out of their classroom as soon as Miss Carson let them go, grabbing her coat and not even bothering to put it on.

"Have a good time!" Arthur yelled after her as she dashed across the playground to Dad. Jade waved back at him gratefully.

"Nice day?" Dad asked, giving her a hug. Toby was holding on to Dad's hand and swinging – he wanted to get going too.

"It was fine, but I couldn't stop thinking about Milo. We are still taking him for a walk, aren't we?" Jade asked.

"Caroline hasn't changed her mind?"

"Nope, she sent me a photo of Milo a little while ago, with a message saying he's really looking forward to his walk." Dad held out his phone and Jade sighed happily as she admired the cute picture of Milo, lying on the kitchen floor with his paws in the air. It looked like he was waving at them.

They dashed home first so Jade could drop off her backpack and quickly change into her wellies. Then they went round the corner to Caroline's house. She opened the door with Milo already on his lead.

"He saw me getting out the poo bags," she explained, and then she noticed Toby's shocked face. Jade could see her trying not to laugh. "Sorry!

Milo knows if I get those it means we're going for a walk. So he got all excited. I was going to run up and down the street with him but you're here already! You must have raced home from school."

"We were really excited too," Jade told her, leaning down to stroke Milo, and giggling as he whined and squirmed about. "We couldn't wait…"

"Neither can Milo!"

"We'd better not keep him hanging around any longer," Dad said, smiling. "We're going to head for the woods today. Any last bits of advice we need to know?"

Caroline handed Dad Milo's lead. "Just watch out for squirrels. He's desperate to chase them – make sure you've got a good hold on his lead if he tries to dash off after one."

"Will do!" Dad nodded and grinned at Jade and Toby. "Let's go, you two!"

It felt so good, walking along the pavement with Milo bouncing excitedly beside them. Caroline had explained that she was going to puppy training classes with him, and he was quite good at walking to heel mostly, but sometimes he forgot and tried to pull. Dad had to tug him back gently and tell him to heel.

"There's another dog coming, Dad," Jade pointed out as they turned into the road where the path through the woods began.

Dad nodded and Jade saw him take a firm grip on the lead. "Thanks, love.

Caroline said Milo was very friendly
with other dogs – but sometimes you
don't know how the other dog's feeling!"

Luckily the dog coming towards
them was an elderly looking spaniel
with huge, furry, curly ears. She only
wanted to sniff politely at Milo while he
stood there twitching with excitement,
letting out shy little whining noises.

"What a beautiful puppy," the man walking her said, smiling at Jade and Toby. "Aren't you lucky?"

Jade beamed at him. They must look like proper dog owners then! "We're actually just borrowing him," she explained. "We're taking him for walks to help out his real owner. I wish he did really belong to us."

"That's very kind of you! This is my Sophy's favourite place for a walk. Have a great time!"

"Dog people are nice," Jade said as they started along the path.

Dad nodded. "I think you're right. I suppose if you like dogs, it's good to talk to other people who like them as well."

Jade loved walking in the woods –

there were always things to find, like tiny mushrooms growing on fallen trees, or patches of moss that looked like a little emerald garden. She'd always enjoyed admiring people's dogs too. But now they had Milo with them, everything was different. He kept stopping to sniff at the bracken or an interesting tree and every smell was obviously so exciting. He'd sniff and sniff and his tail wagged so hard that his whole bottom wriggled. It made Toby laugh every time.

Milo was fascinated by the rustling noises from birds up in the trees too. Luckily they only saw one squirrel and it dashed away along a huge branch so fast that he hardly had time to bark at it.

"I think we should probably head back," Dad said at last. "I'm getting hungry for dinner and I bet Milo wants his too. We have to be careful not to tire Milo out – he's very young still."

"He's definitely slowing down," Jade agreed. Milo was still bouncy, his tail swishing happily, but he was now panting a bit too. "Shall we take you home?" she asked, crouching down to rub his soft red-gold muzzle. "Shall we? Are you tired?"

Milo leaned forwards just a little and swept his huge raspberry-pink tongue all down Jade's cheek.

"Ugh." Jade wiped her face and giggled. "But I do love you," she told him. "Even if you're all slobbery."

Milo sat by the door, listening hopefully. It was almost time, he was sure. This was when they came – not every day, but most days. Yes! He could hear footsteps pattering on the path outside. He flung himself at the door, woofing with excitement and scrabbling at the shiny paint.

"You silly boy," Caroline murmured. "Come on. Get down. That's it – no, down! I can't open the door if you're doing that, can I? OK, good boy."

Milo sniffed round the edge of the door as she opened it, wanting to nuzzle at Jade and Toby and lick them and love them all over.

He plunged at Toby, but Caroline

caught hold of his collar. "Careful, Milo! You'll knock him over! Jade, can you hold on to him while I grab his lead? He's been sitting by the door waiting for you."

Milo squeaked as he spotted Caroline getting his lead down from the hook. And he danced around in circles as Jade tried to hold him still for Caroline to clip the lead on.

"You're just excited to go to the beach, aren't you?" Jade said to Milo, as Caroline handed the lead to her.

Milo plunged away down the garden path so quickly that Jade had to scurry to keep up with him.

"Hey, Milo, heel. Walk nicely."

Milo pulled for a moment more – he just wanted to get going! – but the collar hurt his neck when he dragged like that, so he slowed down and padded along more calmly next to Jade.

They were going the other way today, he realized, looking around as they turned out of the garden gate. Until now they'd been to the woods and the big park with the playground but this was different...The beach! They were going to the beach! He could smell the sharp salt air and the faint smell of dead fish and old seaweed and chip wrappers. Milo loved the beach! It was hard not to start pulling again at the thought of it, but he just hurried on a bit faster instead.

"Ooooooh, it's windy!" Jade called as they came to the long flight of

shallow concrete steps that led down
the cliff to the beach.

"Your mum always used to say this
sort of day blew the cobwebs away!"
Dad yelled back. "Watch out for Milo,
Jade. The wind might make him a bit
wild and jumpy."

Milo scurried down the steps, the
wind flapping his ears, and they
raced out on to the shingly beach,
crunching over the pebbles. Milo was
running in big, bounding leaps and
Jade ran beside him, laughing. They
skidded to a stop just in front of the
water, and Milo sniffed at the creamy
foam that was settling on the stones.
It made him sneeze, and he shook his
ears wildly. Jade jumped back with a
squeak as the next wave came lapping

up to her shoes, and Milo bounced
with her, barking excitedly at the sea.
His paws were all wet but he liked it.

Jade crouched down to hug him and Milo nuzzled at her, burying his nose in her wind-wild hair. He wasn't always sure about people hugging him, but Jade was good at knowing when to let go if he tried to squirm away. He'd been waiting all day for this – for her and Toby and their dad.

Toby came stumbling over the pebbles to hold on to the lead next to Jade, and they set off again, galloping along the edge of the water as the waves rushed in and sucked back out. Milo could feel the wind ruffling his fur and the air was full of the strange, good smells of the beach.

He loved it.

Chapter Four

"I wish you could come back to our house with us," Jade whispered to Milo. She was walking a little bit ahead of Dad. Toby was tired and whining about being hungry, so Dad was trying to cheer him up. They'd been to the playground after a walk around the park and Toby had worn himself out clambering over the climbing frame.

Milo looked up at her and Jade sighed. "I love walking you, but it would be so nice to take you home sometimes too. Maybe you could come and sit on my feet while I did my homework. Or ... or we could watch TV together. It's stupid, isn't it? A month ago I'd have said just walking a beautiful dog would make me happy. And now I've got exactly what I wanted but I still want more... Oh well. We're nearly home. Milo, you look just as tired as Toby."

Jade opened Caroline's garden gate, and Milo put on a burst of energy and dashed up the path. Jade could see Caroline waving from the front window. She'd explained that she usually sat there to work. Milo whined happily as he heard her coming to the door.

"Hi, Jade! Nice walk?" Caroline unclipped Milo's lead and he hurried into the house to get a drink from his water bowl.

"It was great! We went to the park." Jade looked round as Dad and Toby came up behind her.

"Actually, would you be able to pop in just for a minute?" Caroline said to Dad. She sounded uncomfortable and Jade glanced worriedly between her and Dad. What was wrong?

"Sure... Is everything OK?" Dad asked. "Milo seemed fine, he's definitely getting better at walking to heel."

"Milo's great. And he loves going

for walks with you, it's nothing like that. Um, look. I'll put the kettle on."

Jade glanced up at Dad. Caroline was clearly upset, and she could tell Dad was anxious. She didn't want to go inside and have tea and find out whatever this news was… If only she'd hurried away as soon as Caroline opened the door…

Biting her lip, Jade followed Dad into the kitchen. She crouched down next to Milo's basket and stroked his nose, and the puppy thumped his tail wearily against the cushion – he was worn out from their walk. Dad said he always walked three times as far as they did because he did so much running backwards and forwards on his long lead.

Toby was still complaining about being hungry so Caroline gave him a chocolate biscuit and he perked up a bit. At last they were all sitting round the table.

"Sorry…" Caroline mumbled. "I've been putting off telling you this, because I didn't really know how to say it. You've been so amazing with Milo, all of you, and he's loved going for walks with you."

"Can't we walk him any more?"
Jade asked, her voice shaking. "I don't
understand…"

"I'm moving," Caroline told her. "I'm
so sorry, Jade. It's my work. The office
is closing and I've had to look for a new
job – and well, I've got one, but it's not
anywhere near here." She gave a sad
little laugh. "Actually, it's in Paris."

"In France?" Dad said, sounding a bit
stunned.

"Yes." Caroline sighed. "I studied
French at university, so it's really
exciting to have a chance to work there.
But it's a big change. I'm really sorry. I
feel like you've just got to know Milo
and now we're leaving."

"Why's Jade crying?" Toby asked
loudly.

Jade hadn't known that she was – she swiped her hand over her face, and Toby was right. Then she felt a soft, damp nose press up against her knee, and she realized that Milo had come to see what was the matter too. He was gazing up at her with his dark eyes, his tail wagging uncertainly.

"Ohhh!" Jade couldn't bear to look at him, it made her too sad. She jumped up from her chair and stumbled through the kitchen to the hallway. She just wanted to get out. She struggled with the front door lock – she could hear Dad behind her apologizing to Caroline and explaining to Toby that they needed to go – but then she finally managed to get the door open and she ran down the path, back to their house.

Jade was sitting
on the front
doorstep with
her chin in her
hands when Dad
and Toby finally
caught up with her.

Dad sighed and
stepped round her to
put the key in the door.
"I suppose I should be cross with you
for running off like that but I'm not,"
he said sadly. "I mean, please don't
do it again, but I know how you feel,
Jade. It was a big shock." He gently
shooed Toby inside, telling him to take
his coat off, and crouched down next
to Jade, putting his arm around her
shoulders. "I'm really sorry."

"Dad. Can we go to the pet shop on the way back to Caroline's? I – I want to get a goodbye present for Milo."

Dad had asked Jade if she wanted to stop walking Milo now – if it would be too sad to keep on seeing him when they knew he was going away to Paris soon. Jade had thought about it, but she couldn't bear not to see the puppy again. They had a few more weeks before Caroline moved and she'd be extra busy packing up her flat. Milo would need them more than ever.

But Jade couldn't look forward to their walks the way she had before. Now she had to remember there would only be a few more of them…

"I made him and Caroline a card at lunchtime," she told Dad. "Miss Carson gave me a piece of card and Arthur helped me – he's really good at drawing. He drew the Eiffel Tower on it and I drew Milo with Caroline." She ducked her head. "Caroline's upset about leaving too and I made her feel worse when she told us. I want to give her the card. And I want Milo to have a present to remember us by. A really nice toy."

"That's a good idea. I'll stay outside with Milo, and you and Toby can choose something." Dad glanced down at Toby doubtfully. Toby hadn't really understood what was happening and Dad had told Jade he wasn't sure whether to tell him or not.

There was a whole shelf of dog toys in the pet shop but in the end Jade chose a squeaky chew toy that was shaped like a red post box. She thought it might remind Milo of his old home – she wasn't sure what colour post boxes were in France but she guessed they would be different.

Jade held out the toy and the card to Caroline as soon as she answered the door – she really had been feeling guilty about running away from her earlier in the week. But as Caroline looked at the picture on the front, and then read the message Jade had written inside, her face crumpled.

"Don't you like it?" Jade whispered.

"It's beautiful – thank you so much for making it for us. And for bringing the lovely present for Milo!" Caroline said, sniffing. "It's just … you put Milo and me there next to the Eiffel Tower, but … Milo's not coming." She made a strange gulping noise that Jade realized was her trying not to cry.

"Not coming…?" Jade echoed.

"No." Caroline was really crying now. "No, he can't. The flat I've got in Paris won't allow dogs. I've looked and looked … I just can't find one anywhere."

"But what's going to happen to Milo?" Dad asked.

"I'm going to ring up the animal shelter and ask them to take him," Caroline said shakily. "I'm hoping it won't be difficult to find a new home for him since he's so young."

"Oh…" Dad nodded but he looked shocked – almost as shocked as Jade felt. Poor Milo. She had been desperately sad for herself and Dad and Toby before, but now she was feeling awful for him too.

Milo stood next to Caroline in the doorway. His tail was clamped between his legs and he whined. He was sure there was something wrong with Caroline, and now Jade was acting strangely too. Their walk had been slow today – Jade hadn't wanted to race along the paths with him, like she usually did. He'd trotted round her in circles, trying to cheer her up and get her to run, but she'd only sniffed and patted him.

Milo could feel everyone's unhappiness buzzing around them. He didn't understand what was happening, but he knew he didn't like it. He nudged his muzzle softly against Caroline's knee and she crouched down to stroke him. She was making sad noises and her breathing was all hitched up inside her. Milo licked her cheek anxiously, desperate to make her feel better.

"Oh, you're such a good boy…" Caroline whispered. "I'm so sorry, Milo. I really am."

Milo gazed at her worriedly, wondering what was going on. His tail was even further between his legs now and his ears were flattened. Why was everyone so unhappy?

Chapter Five

"Are you OK?" Arthur asked, leaning across the table while they waited for Miss Carson to do the register on Monday morning.

Jade blinked at him uncertainly.

"You just look a bit … weird." Arthur frowned at her. "Have you got a cold?"

Jade shook her head. She didn't have a cold but she'd been crying. All weekend, it felt like, although she knew that couldn't really be true. But every time she'd thought about Milo, or about the beach, or the woods, tears had come pricking at the backs of her eyes, and her throat felt sticky and strange. Everything seemed to make her cry. And Dad was miserable too. He still hadn't told Toby what was happening and her little brother being so happy and normal just made Jade feel worse.

"She's been crying," Lola said, eyeing Jade with her head on one side.

Jade sighed. Lola shared their table. She was nice but she wasn't very tactful. She blurted everything out. "Thanks," she muttered.

"Oh, sorry…" Lola looked embarrassed. "What's wrong, Jade?"

"Milo…" Jade swallowed hard. "The puppy we've been helping to look after. His owner's got a new job in Paris."

Arthur made a face. "You'll really miss him." Arthur had a dog too, a huge lurcher called Kenny. His mum brought Kenny to pick Arthur up sometimes. He was taller than most of the little ones in Reception but he was really friendly. He liked watching TV, and when she'd gone round to Arthur's house, Jade had sat on the sofa with Arthur and his little brother Sam, all three of them leaning against Kenny like a big furry grey cushion.

Arthur had told her that his mum and dad had got Kenny from an animal shelter, and Kenny had hated it there. One of the reasons they'd chosen him was because he'd stopped bothering to look at any of the people who came past him wanting a dog. He was too big and too scary and he'd cost too much to feed – that was what everyone had thought. So Kenny had given up. He thought no one would ever want to take him home. He'd made Arthur's mum cry right there in the shelter, and she and Arthur's dad had adopted him that same day. Arthur's mum made Kenny a cake out of dog food on his adoption day every year.

"It's worse than that," Jade whispered. "She can't take Milo with her. He's got to go to the shelter."

Arthur's mouth dropped open but Lola looked confused. "Why doesn't she just let you keep him?"

Jade sighed. It was exactly what she'd been wishing all weekend. "I'd love it if we could. But we only signed up to that website because Toby's too little for us to have a dog of our own, and Dad's got enough to do already. Dad says maybe when we're older but it's not a good idea now…"

Arthur shook his head. "We've had Kenny since before I was born. Mum says he used to help her rock my Moses basket when I was a baby. And I know he was brilliant with Sam, I saw! Kenny used to pick him up by the back of his jumper if Sam was trying to eat his food! Sam tries to eat everything…"

"Jade's dad's only being sensible," Lola argued. "What if Toby pulled the puppy's tail or something? He might get bitten."

"I don't think Milo would bite," Jade said, her voice wobbling. "He's really friendly. But that's the sort of thing Dad says too."

"He is friendly," Arthur said encouragingly. "And he's really sweet. He won't be at the shelter long, Jade. Everyone's going to want to adopt him."

"I know…" Jade sniffed. She could feel the tears pressing behind her eyes again, and she'd been trying so hard not to cry. "How could anyone not want him? But he's going to be so confused. He loves his owner Caroline and he loves us and now he's not going to see any of us ever again!"

"Maybe you could visit him?" Lola suggested, not sounding very hopeful.

"Maybe…" Jade whispered, but she wasn't feeling hopeful either.

Milo sat in his basket, watching Caroline as she reached into the backs of the kitchen cupboards, muttering to herself. The kitchen was full of big cardboard boxes, so many that Milo had to thread his way through them if he wanted to get to his water bowl.

He didn't like it.

What was Caroline doing? She kept putting things into the boxes, and then taking them out again, and making tall, dusty piles. It wasn't just in the kitchen either. There were suitcases in the hallway and more boxes in the little living room. Things weren't where they ought to be any more.

Milo got up and went to sniff at the boxes again. He kept doing it because he was hoping things might have gone back to the way they were. But every time the piles were bigger and the boxes were fuller.

He wriggled in between two boxes and squeezed out into the hallway. More bags had arrived and most of the coats had disappeared off the hooks on the wall. His lead was still hanging up there, though. Milo gazed up at it sadly. He hadn't had much of a walk today. Caroline still seemed edgy and upset, and she'd hurried him round the park so fast he'd hardly had time to sniff all his favourite smells.

Milo slunk into the living room. He liked to curl up in here in the evenings

with Caroline. She let him sit on the
sofa with her, and there was a big, soft
cushion for him too. Except now the
cushion was in a big bag in the corner
of the room, which wasn't where it was
supposed to be at all. Milo went to look
at it, scrabbling to catch the edge of the
bag with his front paws. The fabric was
stiff and crackly but he squished it a bit
so he could just manage to peer over the
edge. His cushion was in there and all
his toys. His grooming brush and his
coat that he wore on walks sometimes.
The bag was almost full. There was a
packet of dog treats in there too, the
stick-shaped ones that he really liked.

Milo looked round to see if Caroline
was still in the kitchen. He had a feeling
he wasn't supposed to know about

those treats. But she was busy in there
– he could hear her banging things
around. Swiftly he reached into the bag,
wiggling a bit so he could get further in
and snag the packet of treats. Then he
hurried behind the sofa and started to
chew through the silvery packet with his
sharp puppy teeth.

He ate the lot.

Jade lay on her bed, listening to Dad read Toby a story in his room next door. She was drawing another picture of Milo – not looking jaunty and happy by the Eiffel Tower this time but slumped flat, his nose resting on a hard floor. She knew that animal shelters were probably a lot nicer than in her drawing. They were full of people who loved cats and dogs and were desperate to find them the best new homes. But she couldn't help imagining Milo alone and miserable, missing Caroline, missing *them*.

She started to draw a wire fence in front of the red-gold puppy, a bit like a cage, but it made her feel so sad that she only managed a couple of lines.

"Are you going to have a bath?" Dad asked, popping his head round the door. "Oh, are you still finishing your homework? I thought you'd done it all."

"I did. It's just a picture…"

Dad came in properly and picked up Jade's drawing. Then he sat down next to her on the bed and sighed.

"I know it's hard, sweetheart. But I'm sure Milo's going to find a lovely home. People often want young dogs when they go to an animal shelter and Milo's very friendly. We've made sure he's used to families as well! Caroline took him to training classes and puppy parties, so he's good with other dogs. He's pretty much perfect. And…" He hesitated and Jade looked up at him.

"What?"

"Well … in a little while, maybe
we'll feel like finding another dog to
look after through the website."

Jade stared at her dad, wide-eyed.
She hadn't even thought about it. How
could they? After Milo, who was so

sweet and loving and just perfect? She couldn't imagine ever wanting to spend time with another dog.

She turned away from him, pulling her drawing out of his hands and huddling up against the wall.

"No, thank you," she muttered. She was trying not to sound angry – but she was. She was furious. How could Dad even think of it? Didn't he care about Milo at all?

Chapter Six

This might be the last time we come to the park with Milo.

It kept echoing inside Jade's head. Caroline was leaving for Paris in a fortnight, she'd said, but she hadn't yet contacted the animal shelter about giving Milo up. Jade had a feeling she was putting it off. Caroline had looked uncomfortable when Dad asked her about it and changed the subject. Jade could understand. She didn't want to say goodbye to Milo – she could hardly bear to think about it. But it must be so much worse for Caroline, who had known him longer and had expected to keep him forever.

Although … Caroline did have the excitement of moving to a new place that would be so different and strange. Jade, Toby and Dad would be here at home where everything would be the same, just without Milo.

Jade caught her breath in surprise as Milo jumped up, putting his paws on her knees and gazing up at her. He whined quietly – almost as though he was asking her what was the matter.

"You're so clever," Jade murmured,

reaching down and rubbing his head and ears lovingly. "You know when someone's sad, don't you? Don't worry, Milo. Everything's going to be OK. You're going to have a lovely new home, I know you will." She sniffed, and her shoulders drooped. She was trying to sound cheerful but it was hard work. "I didn't mean to spoil your walk," she said, giving herself a little shake. It was just – she kept remembering the story Arthur had told her about Kenny in the shelter. It wasn't that the people there hadn't looked after Kenny. They'd done everything they could – there was nice food, and volunteers who came in to take the dogs out for walks and brought in special toys. But Kenny had still hated it. He'd known it wasn't a proper home for a dog, even though he'd never really had one. She couldn't bear to think of Milo in a pen, lonely and miserable. He'd know that Caroline had left him behind, that she and Dad and Toby didn't want him… Which made it all so much worse, because she did want him, she really did!

"I don't want to walk!" Toby howled from behind her and Jade sighed. Toby could tell that she and Dad were unhappy, just like Milo could.

He'd been complaining and dragging his feet pretty much since they set off from Caroline's. Usually he loved being out on a long walk, especially if Dad gave him a piggyback towards the end when he was getting tired. But today he'd whinged and moaned, and now he was just standing in the middle of the path with his fists clenched and his face screwed up and scarlet.

"Do you want a piggyback?" Dad asked gently.

"Nooooo! I want to go home. I want home now!"

"We can't do that," Dad tried to explain. "We're in the middle of the park and we've got to take Milo back before we can go home."

"Home now!"

Dad looked up at the sky. Jade had a feeling he was counting in his head, so he didn't say something cross to Toby. That would just make things worse.

"I know you're tired, Tobes. Have a piggyback. We'll go down this path – it'll take us to Caroline's house and it goes past the playground. Do you want a go on the swings?"

Toby opened his eyes cautiously. "The slide?" he asked. "Want to take Rabbit on the slide!" He held up his saggy old rabbit toy to Dad.

"Sure, if that's what you want. Jade can go with you, or I can, and then Jade can sit with Milo for a bit."

"You!" Toby demanded and Dad

looked round at Jade.

"Is that OK, Jade?"

Jade nodded. She was feeling tired too. She hadn't slept very well the night before – she'd woken up from a weird dream where she could hear Toby and Milo somewhere in the dark, and she couldn't find either of them. It had been horrible and she'd sat hugging her knees in bed for ages before she'd dared to try and go back to sleep. She wouldn't mind sitting on the grass just outside the playground for a while, cuddling up with Milo.

Milo lay down beside Jade, panting happily in the warm spring sunshine.

He was glad to be out of the flat. Nothing was where it was meant to be, and there seemed to be more boxes and bags piled up every day. He kept losing his toys and last night he'd chewed a hole in the corner of one of the boxes because the cardboard was tough and felt good to gnaw on with his sore puppy gums. Caroline had caught him at it and hustled him away, and he knew she was cross and worried.

He shuffled closer to Jade and buried his nose in her ear, which made her giggle. He liked that noise. Jade had been quiet the last few days when they were out for walks – they hadn't done any wild laughing runs along the beach or through the woods. He loved it when Jade raced as joyfully as he did. A few times today, when the wind was ruffling up his fur, he'd looked round at her hopefully, wishing they could dash away together. But Jade had been plodding along with her head hanging or staring sadly into the distance. He'd known it wasn't the time.

Jade lay back on the grass with her arm around him. "You're so soft," she whispered, and she sounded sleepy. Milo snuffled happily, settling down on the grass next to her and wriggling so that his nose was shoved up under Jade's chin. That was good. Jade was warm and she was comfy to lie on. His eyes fluttered half closed and Milo settled into a doze.

"Are you two OK?" Dad asked,
laughing, and Jade blinked up at him.
"I think you're asleep!"

"No, I'm not," Jade said, propping
herself up on her elbows and trying not
to yawn. "OK, maybe I was a bit asleep.
Milo was so warm and snuggly…"

"It's fine. I just came to make sure
you've got Milo's lead wrapped tightly

round your wrist, that's all. We don't want him wandering off. Though actually he looks even sleepier than you…"

Dad smiled down at the puppy, who thumped his tail slowly on the grass, and then sniffed Dad's fingers. Dad crouched down to give him a stroke.

"You're a good boy, aren't you?" he said quietly. "Having a nice rest and looking after Jade for me, that's right. Good dog. Are you feeling better, Jade? You looked tired this morning."

Jade nodded, and yawned again, and then she sat up properly. Something had been niggling at her and now she realized what it was. She was looking at the playground and she couldn't see Toby. She couldn't see any small person

in a bright red coat. Jade scanned the
playground again, pausing for a second
as she caught a flash of red, but it was
only a little girl running across the
grass in scarlet wellies.

"Dad! Where's Toby?"

"Don't worry, he's on the scramble net. You know he loves trying to get up there." Dad turned to look back at the playground, and Jade saw his shoulders stiffen as he realized what she'd already seen.

Toby wasn't on the scramble net, or the ladder up to the slide, or the bouncing mat. He wasn't anywhere in the playground at all. He was gone.

Chapter Seven

Milo jumped up, trotting after Jade and Dad. He wasn't sure why they seemed so upset, but he could tell from their sharp, anxious voices that something was very wrong. Jade was holding on to his lead too tightly, so that it dragged at his neck. He pulled back a little, but she didn't seem to notice.

"Toby! Toby! Where are you?" Jade called, her voice rising high with panic.

Toby... Yes, where was he? Usually he was with Dad, holding his hand as they walked along, never far away. Milo looked around the park, confused. Toby should be here with them. He was always here...

Milo knew that Toby was only small. He was younger than Jade and he couldn't walk as far. He stumbled sometimes and Dad and Jade looked after him. Milo was sure that he was supposed to look after Toby too, and he hadn't. They had let him slip away out of sight.

It was Milo's job to find him.

"He was on the scramble net. I only left him for two minutes to come and check on you and Milo. He can't have gone!" Dad was by the gate into the fenced playground, with Jade and Milo standing next to him. He was turning round in a circle as though he didn't know which direction to look in first. Jade had never seen him look so panicked – not even when she'd fallen down the stairs a couple of years before and broken her arm.

"He can't have come out of the playground," Jade said, still scanning the play equipment. "There's a gate. He couldn't open that, could he?"

Dad's face brightened. "No, you're right, I don't think he could. But I can't see him, unless… Maybe he's hiding!"

He unfastened the gate and hurried in while Jade leaned as far over the fence as she could, trying to spot Toby. There were so many places he might have hidden, that was the problem. Both the

slides had those little cabins at the top and there was a tunnel as part of the climbing frame. Plus there were all the trees…

"Dad! Maybe behind that tree?" Jade waved at Dad and pointed, and he hurried to look. But he came back shaking his head. He was looking more and more worried.

"Excuse me – you couldn't just open the latch on the gate for me, could you?" someone called, and Jade glanced round. She'd been so busy watching Dad that she hadn't spotted a lady approaching the gate from inside the playground with two small children – a girl about Toby's age and a baby. She was trying to manage a double pushchair and the little girl's scooter, and she just didn't have enough hands to open the gate.

"Oh, sure, sorry!" Jade went to open it for her, sliding back the bolt and holding the gate open to let the pushchair through. Toby definitely couldn't have done that, she told herself, feeling relieved. The bolt was high up on the gate and it was quite stiff. He just wouldn't have been able to pull it.

But as the lady was saying thank you and coaxing her little girl out of the gate, Jade noticed another child running up behind them. The first family didn't see him at all, the mum was fussing over the baby, who had started to cry, and the little girl was trundling off on her scooter. The small boy nearly made it out of the gate, and Jade was wondering if she ought to stop him – when his mum called him back.

Jade shut the gate and pushed the bolt across with shaky fingers. The playground was busy – it always was after school on a sunny day. It would have been easy for Toby to dart out of the gate behind another family if he'd wanted to. So easy.

Dad was nearly back with them now.

She was going to have to tell him what had happened. But as he undid the bolt, Jade realized he'd seen it too.

"I think Toby might have followed some other children out…" she whispered and Dad nodded as he pulled the gate open.

"I saw that little boy nearly running out. Hey! Jade, don't let Milo in there, no dogs in the playground!"

Jade tried to catch the lead, but she'd been so distracted watching Dad search that she hadn't been holding on very tightly, and it slipped through her fingers. Milo darted through the gate before she could stop him.

"Milo, come back!" Jade yelped. But the puppy ignored her. He ran across the playground, ignoring the worried looks from a few parents. He was making straight for the slide, rooting about for something in the long tufts of grass by the ladder. Jade and Dad rushed after him.

"Milo, what are you doing?" Dad said. "We can't mess around now, we need to be searching the rest of the park for Toby. Come on!"

"Dad, look!" Jade crouched down, grabbing hold of Milo's trailing lead. "Look what Milo's got!" Milo sat back proudly and gazed up at Jade and her dad. There in the grass was Toby's old Rabbit.

"You clever dog!" Jade said, picking Rabbit up. "Did you know that we were looking for Toby?"

"He *is* clever," Dad said. "I know Caroline told us he was very good in his puppy training classes, but I didn't expect him to do something like this. I wonder…" He took the tatty rabbit from Jade and turned it over in his hands.

"Dad, do you think Milo could look for Toby?" Jade asked hopefully. "Could he sniff him out? He's trying to find him, I'm sure he is!"

"That's what I was thinking too," Dad agreed. "It's worth a try. But he's going to have to be quick, Jade. I know Toby's only been gone a few minutes, but if we don't find him soon, I think I'm going to have to call the police. We need help."

Jade nodded, shivering a little, even though the sun was shining. She'd been thinking they'd find Toby any moment now – that he'd come racing out from behind one of the trees, or shooting down the slide, laughing because he'd tricked them so well. Talking about the police made it all sound much more serious.

She took Rabbit out of Dad's hands and held him in front of Milo. "Where's Toby?" she asked. "Can you find Toby, Milo?" She looked hopefully at the puppy, who was gazing back at her with bright, intelligent eyes. He did look clever – but he was so little too. Perhaps too little to do something so important and difficult. Were they asking too much?

Milo obviously didn't think so. He sniffed thoughtfully at the toy rabbit, and then looked about for a moment. Then he set off, tugging determinedly on his lead, and made for the playground gate.

He was tracking Toby, Jade was sure of it.

Milo padded through the grass, sniffing every so often. Rabbit smelled so strongly of Toby, it was almost as if he could see the little boy in front of him. The scent was quite clear. He'd left the playground and headed into the park along a different path, not the one they'd walked down today. It was familiar, though. They'd definitely been there before, Milo remembered it.

"Are we sure he's right about this?" Dad murmured anxiously. "He could be taking us in completely the wrong direction."

"He knows, Dad, look at him!" Jade protested. "He keeps stopping to sniff. I'm sure he's got Toby's scent."

Milo snuffled at the grass. Yes, there it was again, clear as anything. He sped up, hurrying along the path, until it split in two, one fork leading to the lake, and the other one to the gate out into the street. Milo stopped, trying to catch the scent again. He wasn't quite sure…

"That path leads to the road," Dad
said, his voice thin and worried. "Jade,
we can't wait any longer, I need to call
the police. Just hold tight to Milo, OK?"

Milo's head went up. There! Yes,
that was definitely the right scent.
He hurried purposefully away down
the lake path, pulling Jade after him.

Chapter Eight

"I think Toby's gone to the lake, Dad!" Jade yelled, as Milo scampered off down the path. "Let's just see if he's there before you call. You know he loves looking at the ducks!"

Dad hurried after them, frowning worriedly. "But Toby knows he mustn't go near the water by himself. I don't think he'd do that…"

"Milo seems pretty sure, though!"
Jade called back. Milo was going
faster now, eagerly pulling on his
lead. As they came out between the
tall clumps of bushes and spotted the
sunlight glittering on the lake, he let
out an excited yipping noise and sped
up even more.

"He does look as though he knows
what he's doing," Dad muttered,
jogging along beside Jade. "Please be
right about this, Milo…"

They stopped on the path that
ran round the edge of the lake, Milo
sniffing busily and Dad staring grimly
at the water.

"Where's Toby, Milo?" Jade asked
again, holding Rabbit out in front of
the little dog. "Find him for us!"

Milo hardly seemed to need Rabbit at all now. He gave the toy one brief sniff and trotted off along the path again, towards the green-painted building by the edge of the lake.

"The ice-cream hut!" Jade gasped, starting to run. They did come and get ice creams here sometimes as a treat. Toby loved it – he always wanted a cone with strawberry sauce, even though he didn't usually manage to eat it all and Dad had to finish it up for him.

The hut stood on a concrete patio with picnic tables so that everyone could watch the ducks while they were eating their ice cream or drinking tea. There were families with children sitting at two of the tables, an elderly

couple with mugs of tea – and a little
boy in a bright red coat, looking at the
pictures of ice cream on the front of
the hut.

"Toby!" Dad picked him up and hugged him close, so tight that Toby squirmed and squeaked, but he didn't seem to mind that much. He put a hand on Dad's cheek and asked hopefully, "Ice cream?"

"We probably shouldn't, in case he tries this again," Dad said to Jade. "But right now – yes, Tobes, you can have an ice cream."

"Strawberry sauce!"

"Yes, strawberry sauce. Jade, do you want mint choc chip? And well done,

112

sweetheart, for listening to Milo. I can't believe he found Toby. He's amazing."

"Dad, can Milo have my ice cream? I mean, can we get him one instead?" Jade asked. "Look, it says they do special dog ice creams!"

Dad laughed. "We can definitely stretch to an ice cream for Milo as well. He deserves it!"

They sat down at one of the picnic tables by the water, with Toby on Dad's knee. Jade opened up the little tub of doggie ice cream for Milo – it wasn't actually ice cream, she realized, after she read the side. It was a sort of frozen yoghurt with banana, because real ice cream wasn't good for dogs. But Milo seemed to think it was fabulous. After a couple of confused sneezes when he wasn't sure about the cold, he lapped it up eagerly. Jade had to hold the little tub for him because he kept accidentally pushing it around with his nose. She had her ice cream in one hand and Milo's in the other.

"Toby, did you come all the way to the ice-cream hut by yourself?" Dad asked.

"Mmmf." Toby wasn't very clear, since he was quite deep into his ice cream.

"You mustn't go off on your own," Dad said softly. "We were really worried. We didn't know where you were."

"They said ice cream," Toby explained, looking up at Dad for a moment. He pointed to one of the other families, a mum and two girls a little older than he was.

"They were in the playground before," Jade said quietly to Dad. "I bet they were talking about going to get an ice cream and Toby decided he wanted one too. So he followed them."

"Oh wow…" Dad heaved a sigh. "Toby, next time you want an ice cream, you ask me, OK? Don't ever go off with anyone else. Or follow them. You stay with me and Jade!"

"And Milo!" Toby agreed, slurping more of his ice cream.

Dad laughed. "Yes, and Milo. Maybe we should just set Milo to watch you all the time…" He went silent after that, watching Milo licking out the last little traces of dog ice cream from the tub.

Jade looked up at him. "Dad…" she whispered. "Dad, you know you said we couldn't have a dog because Toby's too little?"

Dad nodded. He was still watching Milo, and Jade was sure she could *see* him thinking. It was like there were little wheels clicking round and round in his head.

"I'm starting to realize that maybe I was wrong," he said slowly. "Maybe a dog is just what we need."

"So … can we keep him?" Jade pleaded.

"Maybe … yes. We'll have to talk to Caroline."

"She'd love it! She'd know that Milo was going to have a home with people who love him! People he already knows! And he wouldn't even have to go to the shelter." Jade leaned down to rub her hands over Milo's soft, feathery ears, and the puppy gazed back at her happily, swiping his huge pink tongue around his muzzle to get the last bits of ice cream. "You could come home with us," she told him. "You could be our dog."

Milo leaned over to lick her hands and then his ears twitched. Toby had nearly finished his ice cream and he'd wriggled down from Dad's lap to feed the very end of his cone to the ducks. Milo was watching him – clearly making sure he was safe and not about to wander off again.

"He really is guarding Toby," Jade said.

"I know. He's amazing," Dad agreed. "But, hey – we need to take him back to Caroline now, it's getting late."

"Can we talk to her about adopting him, Dad, please?" Jade begged.

Dad nodded. "Yes. I'd been thinking about it anyway. Milo's become so much a part of our family, I couldn't imagine just letting him go. But now I'm sure adopting him is the right thing to do." He smiled at Jade. "Let's head back to Caroline's."

"You look happy," Caroline said, as she opened the door of her flat.

Caroline didn't, Jade thought. She was trying to smile but she looked tired and there was a streak of dust down the side of her cheek. It was more that she seemed sad, though, especially when she bent down to take off Milo's lead. She rubbed her hand slowly over the back of his head and Jade was sure she sighed.

"Yes, actually." Dad was carrying Toby now, and he hitched him up a bit. "We've been thinking…"

"Please can we adopt Milo?" Jade burst out.

Caroline straightened up, staring at them. "But – but – you said you couldn't have a dog… That was why you signed up for Love My Pup – because of Toby being so little."

120

"I really thought we couldn't," Dad agreed. "I was wrong, though. Toby adores Milo and he's really careful and gentle with him. We'd have to make sure we didn't leave them alone together, but Milo's so good – you've done wonders training him. I've been going over and over it in my head, wondering if it was a good idea, and then today…" Dad sighed, and pressed his cheek into Toby's flyaway hair.

"Toby wandered off but Milo found him for us," Jade explained. "He found Toby's toy rabbit and then he tracked him like a sniffer dog. It was amazing."

Caroline looked anxiously at Toby. "Is he OK?"

Dad smiled. "Toby's fine. He just wanted to go and get an ice cream.

It was my fault for not watching him carefully enough."

"This is just the best news." Caroline crouched down to stroke Milo, who was staring up at her, and started to laugh. "Oh my goodness. I've been so worried about him! I was supposed to call the shelter today – it's at the top of my list of things to get done but I just kept finding excuses not to. I couldn't imagine giving Milo up to strangers."

"We'll look after him," Jade told her. "We really will."

"I know…" Caroline's voice shook. "He has the best time with you – he's always so excited for his walks. Oh, Milo, I think you're going to be the most loved puppy ever."

Milo yawned and stretched, rolling on to his back and waving his paws in the air. He was very comfortable, half on the sofa and half stretched across Jade's lap. Jade reached down and rubbed his tummy, which was exactly what he'd wanted.

"You look so silly," Jade said lovingly. "Silly dog."

"He's a *good* dog," Toby said firmly.

"He can be a good dog and a silly dog at the same time, Toby, don't worry," Dad said from the other end of the sofa.

Milo opened one eye to peer thoughtfully at Dad. Did he look like he was about to move any time soon?

It felt like it ought to be dinnertime, but no one seemed to have noticed. It wasn't that he was *very* hungry yet, but he might be in a minute. Milo sighed gustily and closed his eyes again. Jade was still stroking his tummy and Toby was gently holding one of his back paws while he leaned against Jade. They'd been for a long walk along the beach. Jade had spent ages throwing a ball for him in their little garden. His garden. Dinner was going to happen in a bit…

Milo still remembered Caroline, and he missed her, but he belonged here now. Forever. He knew it, deep down. He was Jade's dog and Toby's and Dad's.

This home was his home too.

From MULTI-MILLION best-selling author

Holly Webb

The
Frightened
Puppy

Illustrated by Sophy Williams

Out Now

From MULTI-MILLION best-selling author

Holly Webb

The
**Smallest
Kitten**

Illustrated by Sophy Williams

HOLLY WEBB

Holly Webb started out as a children's
book editor and wrote her first series for
the publisher she worked for. She has been
writing ever since, with over one hundred
and fifty books to her name. Holly lives
in Berkshire, with her husband and three
children. Holly's pet cats are always
nosying around when she is trying
to type on her laptop.

For more information
about Holly Webb visit:

www.holly-webb.com